# THE Case OF THE Gasping Garbage

DOYLE · AND · FOSSEY

science detectives

THE **Case**

OF
THE **Gasping**

**Garbage**

Michele Torrey

illustrated by
Barbara Johansen Newman

DUTTON CHILDREN'S BOOKS

NEW YORK

Text copyright © 2001 by Michele Torrey
Illustrations copyright © 2001 by Barbara Johansen Newman

*Library of Congress Cataloging-in-Publication Data*
Torrey, Michele.
The case of the gasping garbage / by Michele Torrey; illustrated
by Barbara Johansen Newman.—1st ed.
p.   cm.—(Doyle and Fossey, science detectives)
Summary: Fifth-graders Drake Doyle and Nell Fossey combine
their detective and scientific-investigation skills to solve a variety
of cases, involving a noisy garbage can, endangered frogs, a stuck
truck, and a mysterious love letter. Includes a section of scientific
experiments and activities.
ISBN 0-525-46657-6
[1. Science—Methodology—Fiction. 2. Mystery and detective
stories.] I. Johansen Newman, Barbara, ill.   II. Title.
PZ7.T645725 Cas 2001   [Fic]—dc21   00-058751

Published in the United States 2001 by Dutton Children's Books,
a division of Penguin Putnam Books for Young Readers
345 Hudson Street, New York, New York 10014
www.penguinputnam.com

Designed by Richard Amari
Printed in USA
First Edition
1  3  5  7  9  10  8  6  4  2

To my brother, John,
for all the "tough toenails" and "holy cows"

And to my nieces and nephew,
Melinda, Jennelyn, Adrienne, Eleanor, and Ryan,
mad scientists in the making

M.T.

To my husband, Phil,
my lifelong partner in crime

B.J.N.

# CONTENTS

# THE **Case**
## OF THE **Gasping**
# **Garbage**

## CHAPTER ONE

## MONSTER MISSION

**I**ntroducing Doyle and Fossey.

Science Detectives. Known throughout the fifth grade for their relentless pursuit of answers. And not just any answers. The right answers.

On a damp, drizzly day, in an attic not too far away, Drake Doyle worked alone in his homemade laboratory. The laboratory was filled with the latest scientific equipment: a chalkboard, racks of test tubes, flasks and beakers, dozens of sharpened pencils, and a lab coat with his name on it.

Drake's hair was quite wild (some would say it stuck straight up) and the color of toast. Cinnamon toast, that is. And perched on the end of his nose was a pair of round glasses, making him look very scientific indeed. Which, of course, he was.

On this damp, drizzly day, an experiment was under way. A very important experiment.

The solution in the test tube fizzed and popped.

Drake Doyle glanced at his watch, then scribbled the results in his lab notebook.

*Fizzed and popped.*

*Right on time.*

*Not a second late.*

*EXperIment a SUCCESS.*

Drake slapped his notebook shut. (Serious scientists always slap their notebooks shut.) He shoved his pencil behind his ear just as the phone rang. "Doyle and Fossey," he answered, speaking in his best scientific voice. Nell Fossey was Drake's lab partner. They were in business together. Serious business. Their business card read:

DOYLE AND FOSSEY:
science detectives
CALL US. ANYTIME. 555-7822

"Hurry! Hurry! It's a major emergency!" someone screamed on the other end of the phone. "There's a monster in my garbage can!"

Drake pushed up his glasses with his finger. Obviously, this was an important phone call. Very important. And important phone calls were more important than important experiments. He set his test tubes aside. "Who is this?" he asked.

"Gabby Talberg," she shrieked. "Hurry! Hurry!"

"Oh, hi, Gabby." Gabby Talberg was in Drake's fifth-grade class at school. She was a nice girl, even if she did talk too much. "Now, calm down and speak slowly. What seems to be the problem?"

"Speak-slowly?-Are-you-nuts?-I-said-there's-a-huge-giant-bloodsucking-monster-in-my-garbage-can-and-it's-growing-bigger-and-bigger-every-second-and-I'm-alone-in-the-house-and-it's-going-to-gobble-me-up-and-I-don't-want-to-be-someone's-dinner!" Gabby gasped for breath.

Drake was excited. This could prove to be a great day for Doyle and Fossey, Science Detectives. They'd never had a monster assignment before. And, of course, it would be a great day for the small town of Mossy Lake. They'd publish their findings in the local newspaper. GARBAGE-EATING MONSTER DISCOVERED! MOSSY LAKE'S GARBAGE PROBLEMS SOLVED!

Maybe they'd even lecture at Mossy Lake University!

But Drake couldn't allow his excitement to overwhelm his good scientific sense. That was the first rule of science. And Drake was a stickler about rules of science. He cleared his throat and forced himself to speak calmly. "What makes you think there's a monster?" he asked.

"All kinds of weird gasping noises are coming from my garbage can. Something's inside. Hurry, Drake, you have to come over immediately and get rid of it. Because if you don't, I'll just have to call James Frisco."

Great Scott! thought Drake, horrified. Not James Frisco! Frisco was in their fifth-grade class at school. Frisco was a competitor. Frisco was a scientist, but he was a bad scientist. A very bad scientist. A mad scientist, you might say.

Frisco's business card read:

Why was Frisco such a ~~bad~~ mad scientist? Because if Frisco didn't like a number, he erased it. Because if an experiment asked for pink, Frisco used blue. Because if an experiment called for two, Frisco used one. (Or three.) But most especially, because if an experiment said "Adult Supervision Required, OR ELSE!" Frisco did it anyway. Alone.

Drake knew that if Gabby hired Frisco, there was no telling what could happen. Knowing Frisco's sloppy scientific techniques, Frisco might let the monster out of the can, and he and Gabby would never be seen again! Gobbled in the blink of an eye!

"Drake," said Gabby, "Drake, are you there? I said you have to come over immediately and get rid of it or else I'll call Frisco!"

"Check. I'll be right there."

*Click.*

Drake phoned Nell. She was the most fabulous partner an amateur scientist and detective genius could have. Whenever they had a serious case, Nell dropped everything and reported for duty.

"Doyle and Fossey," she answered, picking up the phone on its first ring.

"Drake here. Meet me at Gabby's house right away. Gabby's garbage is gasping."

"Right."

*Click.*

Nell was already waiting on Gabby's porch by the time Drake arrived. He wasn't surprised, as she was the fastest runner in the fifth grade. With her coffee-colored hair pulled back in a no-nonsense ponytail, her scientist cap shoved atop her head, and her mouth set in a firm line, she looked ready to take on this most difficult case.

"Afternoon, Scientist Nell."

"Afternoon, Detective Doyle." And so saying, Nell rapped sharply on the door.

Inside Gabby's house, Gabby pointed to a dark corner of the garage. "There," she whispered. "There's the bloodsucking monster. Inside that garbage can. Hurry, get rid of it before it eats us all."

Suddenly, the garbage can gasped.

It trembled.

It burped and yurped.

It belched and yelched.

All in all, it was very scary indeed.

Drake and Nell immediately went to work. They pulled on surgical gloves.

*Snap!*

Gabby edged toward the door. "You're not going to take off the lid, are you?"

"If there's a monster inside," Drake replied, "removing the lid would be most foolish. Now, stand back, we'll take it from here."

They tapped the sides of the can. "Sounds hollow," whispered Nell. She scribbled in her lab notebook and tapped again.

Drake sniffed the air. "Smells like fresh-baked bread," he observed. "Hmm. That reminds me. Ms. Talberg, isn't your dad a baker?"

"The best baker there is," answered Gabby. "He won the blue ribbon last year at the county fair. Why?"

"Just wondering," Drake muttered as he recorded his findings in his lab notebook.

Meanwhile, Nell peered at the garbage can with her magnifying glass. She checked its temperature. She drew diagrams and charts. She was a most effi-cient scientist.

Finally, Drake and Nell stood back and removed their surgical gloves.

*Snap!*

"Well?" asked Gabby.

"Puzzling," said Drake.

"Fascinating," said Nell.

Drake pushed up his glasses. "Tell me, Ms. Talberg. Does your garbage can always sit here next to the furnace?"

Gabby shook her head. "My dad moved it a few days ago. Why?"

"It's very warm next to the furnace, that's all," said Drake.

"Eighty-seven degrees, to be precise," added Nell.

"Curious. Very curious," mumbled Drake. He jotted a note to himself in his notebook.

"What are you going to do now?" asked Gabby.

"Nell and I will take the garbage can back to the lab for further analysis. Expect our report within twenty-four hours."

## CHAPTER TWO

## GREAT GASPING GARBAGE!

**D**rake and Nell slogged through mud puddles, lugging the garbage can between them. For a monster, it wasn't very heavy. Even so, Drake slipped and almost fell because his glasses had fogged. Nell helped him up and brushed him off. She was a great partner. (And besides, she was his best friend.)

Finally, they pushed the garbage can through Drake's back door, dragged it up two flights of stairs, and into the attic lab. They set the garbage can in a corner next to a heater. "We must simulate the same environment," said Drake.

"Eighty-seven degrees, to be precise," said Nell.

Drake cleaned his glasses and put on his white lab

coat. Nell did, too, except she didn't have any glasses to clean. They stuck sharpened pencils behind their ears, sat on stools, and opened their lab notebooks. Drake pulled a book off the shelf and shuffled through it until he found the right page. It read: "Monster Analysis: What to do when your garbage is gasping."

Just then, Drake's mom poked her head in the lab. Kate Doyle was a fine cook and ran her own catering company from home. Blueberry muffins were her specialty. Now Mrs. Doyle asked if they wanted any hot chocolate with their muffins, seeing that it was such a damp, drizzly day.

"No thanks," Drake said politely. "Just muffins."

"Coffee. Decaf. Black," said Nell. And she shoved a pencil behind her ear. (Nell forgot she already had a pencil behind her other ear.)

"Affirmative," said Drake's mom, and closed the door.

(Real scientists don't drink hot chocolate. Ditto for real detectives. And they were both.)

"Let's go over the facts again," said Nell.

Drake nodded. "Just the facts, ma'am."

Together they pored over their observations.

After a while, Drake's dad stuck his head in the lab. Sam Doyle owned a science-equipment and sup-

·ply company. He regularly brought home used equipment for the lab: computers, microscopes, telescopes, glassware, Bunsen burners—even an old sink that he plumbed with hot and cold water. If either Drake or Nell needed equipment, Mr. Doyle was the man.

Now Mr. Doyle glanced at the rumbling garbage can and told them to be careful.

"We will," said Drake and Nell.

Mr. Doyle rolled his eyes and closed the door.

"What's he think we're going to do?" asked Drake. "Blow up the lab?"

"You did last time," reminded Nell.

"That's beside the point. Now, where were we? Ah, yes. Based on our observations, Scientist Nell, I have formulated a hypothesis. . . ."

All through the evening they worked. Later Mrs. Doyle brought them tomato soup and grilled cheese sandwiches with a pickle on the side. (Mrs. Doyle always cooked from her vegetarian menu whenever Nell was around, because Nell was a vegetarian.) Drake and Nell washed their hands and sat at Drake's desk, knowing they should never eat or drink while conducting experiments. They were top-notch scientists.

After supper, Nell called her mother and asked if she could stay extra late, given that there was no school tomorrow and that they were swamped with experiments and under a deadline. Ann Fossey was a biology professor at Mossy Lake University. Her specialty was wildlife biology. "Goodness gracious sakes alive," exclaimed Professor Fossey. "Sounds like you're a busy scientist. Now, don't you worry about a thing, my dear. I'll be sure to feed your rats and lizards."

"And don't forget my snakes and bugs."

"Of course, dear," said Professor Fossey. "I'll leave the light on for you."

Finally, after midnight, just when Nell was on her fourth cup of decaf, they had their answer.

In the morning, Nell hurried back to Drake's house. They called Gabby first thing. "Meet us in the lab," said Nell. "We've discovered the identity of the monster."

After Gabby arrived, Drake paced the floor while Nell sat on a stool. "You see, Ms. Talberg," Drake was saying, "it's really quite simple. Nell?"

"Thank you, Detective Doyle. First of all," said Nell, "the garbage can sounded hollow when we tapped on it. Second, the garbage can wasn't too heavy."

"You see, Ms. Talberg," said Drake, "most monsters are quite heavy."

"In addition," added Nell, "the garbage can was stored in a very warm environment. We copied that environment in our lab by setting the can next to the heater and checking its temperature. But most important, the garbage can smelled like bread."

"Remember, your dad is a baker," said Drake. "The best baker around, to be exact. Therefore, based on the clues and our observations, I developed an educated guess—what we scientists call a hypothesis. I believed that the monster lurking inside your garbage can was not really a monster at all, but . . ."

"Yes?" asked Gabby, her eyes wide.

"Yeast," said Drake. "Pure and simple yeast."

"Yeast?"

"Yes, yeast. Allow Scientist Nell to explain."

Nell pointed to a chalkboard with her long, wooden pointer. "As I said, the smell of fresh-baked bread was our biggest clue. You see, yeast is used in making bread. Yeasts are tiny plants that eat starches and sugars. They then turn the starches and sugars into alcohol and carbon dioxide gas."

GARBAGE CAN CLUES:
1. Sounded Hollow
2. Wasn't Heavy
3. Warm Environment
4. Smelled Like Bread
5. Gabby's Dad a Baker

"The tiny bubbles in bread," said Drake, "are the result of carbon dioxide gas."

Nell tapped the chalkboard with her pointer. "You see, Gabby, your dad must have thrown away a combination of yeast and flour. Ingredients used in baking bread. Easily purchased at any grocery store."

Drake pushed up his glasses. "With the right amount of moisture—"

"And a warm environment—" added Nell.

"The yeast was able to grow and multiply by feeding on the flour inside the can," finished Drake. "Quite harmless, really. But the yeast produced so much carbon dioxide gas that the garbage can simply had to 'burp' to release some of the gas."

"We tested our hypothesis," said Nell, "with a thorough set of experiments. We examined the yeast under the microscope and grew it in several different mediums. We've positively identified yeast as your culprit. You can be certain there is no monster inside your garbage can."

Naturally, Gabby was a little disappointed. After all, yeast was not as exciting as a bloodsucking monster. She shook their hands anyway for a job well done. "I knew you could do it," she said. "I can't wait to tell all my friends."

Nell handed Gabby their business card. "Call us. Anytime."

Later that day, Drake wrote in his lab notebook:

*Monster analysis a SUCCESS.*

*Hypothesis correct.*

*Received two prize loaves of bread*

*(EXTRA RAISINS, EXTRA NUTS) as payment.*

*Rating on the delicious scale: 10.*

*Paid in full.*

———————

## CHAPTER THREE

## FROG HOLLOW

It was Friday after school when Drake Doyle was once again busy with an important experiment. Test tubes bubbled and beakers boiled.

"Just as I thought," he murmured. "My hypothesis is confirmed." He wiped the fog off his glasses and scribbled in his lab notebook.

Just then there was a knock at the door.

"Come in," said Drake.

Mrs. Doyle popped her head around the door. "You have a visitor," she said. "A wet one." And in trotted Dr. Livingston. Mrs. Doyle closed the door.

Drake put down his notebook. This must be important, he thought. Very important. Nell never sent

Dr. Livingston, unless it was highly important. "Good boy," said Drake. He scratched Dr. Livingston behind his ears. Then he reached inside the pouch that hung from Dr. Livingston's neck.

Drake withdrew a blank sheet of paper. He flicked on a lamp and held the paper over the bulb. Gradually, words appeared.

Detective Doyle,
Meet me at Frog Hollow. ASAP.
Not a moment to lose.
  Signed,
 Naturalist Nell
P.S. Bring umbrella, etc. It's wet.

Drake quickly pulled on his raincoat and boots. He grabbed his umbrella on his way out the back door. "Bye, Mom! I'll be at Frog Hollow with Nell!"

"Affirmative," said Mrs. Doyle. "Be back by suppertime."

Drake closed the door behind him and pushed up his glasses with his finger. He whipped open his umbrella and said, "Follow me" to Dr. Livingston. Drake stepped off the porch into the rain, promptly slipped, and fell with a splat.

Dr. Livingston licked Drake's face.

Drake struggled to his feet, and off they went. Over hill and over dale. Finally they reached Frog Hollow. And there was Nell in her yellow raincoat and naturalist cap. She was examining something with her magnifying glass.

"What is it, Naturalist Nell?" Drake asked, bending down beside her.

Besides being a superb scientist, Nell Fossey was also a naturalist. If it crawled, Nell took notes. If it hopped, Nell followed. If it grew, Nell drew graphs. Nell loved nature. Nature was her specialty.

But today Nell was troubled. Something was wrong—very wrong. "Look here," she said. "This is a leopard frog. In fact, this whole meadow is full of them. But you already knew that."

"Correct," agreed Drake. "That's why it's called Frog Hollow."

"Every spring," Nell continued, "female leopard frogs must find a pond in which to lay their eggs."

"So what's the problem?" asked Drake.

"Follow this frog, and you'll find your answer," replied Nell.

The frog began to hop. Nell and Drake followed, with Dr. Livingston close behind. The frog hopped over a log. It hopped around a rock. It hopped through the tall grass. It hopped and hopped and hopped.

And then something terrible happened.

The frog hopped onto a road, and . . . *ZOOM!* . . . *squish!*

"Eeww," said Drake.

"Ugly," said Nell.

"Woof," said Dr. Livingston.

"Now what do we do?" asked Drake.

"Follow me," said Nell. After looking in both directions, Nell led the way across the road and down the other side. And there, sitting all alone with not a frog in sight, was a pond.

"I think I see the problem," said Drake.

"Indeed," answered Nell. "This road was built just a few months ago. In order for the female frogs to lay their eggs—"

"—they have to cross the road," finished Drake.

"Exactly. And you can see the results for yourself." Nell sighed. "The whole leopard frog population is in danger. If they can't get to the pond, there won't be any new frogs."

"So what can we do?" asked Drake.

Nell set her mouth in a firm line. Drake could tell she was serious. Dead serious. "Come to my house," she said. "My mom's still at work, but I'm sure she won't mind if we make some road signs. We must save the frogs."

"Check," said Drake.

Nell's bedroom was like a jungle. Nature Headquarters, they called it. Terrariums, aquariums, fly traps, and ant farms lined the walls. Paper vines hung from huge papier-mâché trees. A moist, hamster-ish smell of sawdust, fish food, and lizard breath clung to the air. It was even a little steamy. Drake's glasses fogged.

All afternoon they worked. They outlined and colored and glittered and painted. They glued and stapled and taped and hammered. Finally, they were finished.

SLOW DOWN! the signs said. FROG CROSSING! NATURE IN PROGRESS!

"There." Nell nodded with satisfaction. "That should do it."

## CHAPTER FOUR

## TO THE RESCUE!

**B**ut it didn't.

The next day, just as Drake was swirling a solution in a flask, the phone rang.

"Doyle and Fossey," Drake answered.

"It's just terrible," said Nell.

"What is?"

"It's just awful."

"Calm down, Naturalist Nell, and tell me what the problem is."

"It's the road signs. The wind blew them down. And they got all wet. And then the cars ran over them. And no one slowed down. And dozens of frogs have died horrible deaths."

Drake frowned. Once again, Nell was right. This was awful. Just awful. "What are we going to do?" he asked.

"Call all our friends," replied Nell. "Tell them to tune their radios to 98.4 FM at ten A.M."

"Check."

*Click.*

Drake made dozens of phone calls. After all, they had lots of friends.

"Tune your radio to 98.4 FM. Ten A.M. Sharp."

"Check," they answered.

*Click.*

Finally, at ten o'clock, Drake turned on the radio.

The announcer was saying, ". . . And our guest today is Ms. Nell Fossey, Nature's Naturalist. Now tell us, Ms. Fossey, what brings you here today?"

"Frogs."

"What about frogs?"

"Allow me to explain," said Nell. And so she did. She explained about frogs. She explained her observations. She explained the problem. "And finally, if we want to save our frog population, we must build a culvert."

"A culvert?" the announcer asked.

"That's right, a culvert. Dig a tunnel under the

road and right out the other side. That way, the frogs can hop through the culvert, and they won't have to cross the road."

"Hmm . . ." said the announcer. "That sounds expensive. Who's going to pay for this?"

"That's why I'm on the air. Listen up, Mossy Lake. Meet me at the town square at twelve noon tomorrow. We'll rally with signs and take donations."

"Thank you, Ms. Fossey, for this most delightful interview."

"My pleasure," she replied.

Drake flicked off the radio. Great Scott! A culvert! It just might work! Nell was brilliant, absolutely brilliant.

At twelve o'clock sharp, Drake met Nell in the town square. Unlike the day before, it was a bright, beautiful day with cotton-ball clouds and plenty of sunshine. Already dozens of kids were there with their parents.

SAVE THE FROGS! the signs said. SAVE THE TADPOLES! SAY YES TO THE ENVIRONMENT!

Nell put out a jar for money.

The day wore on. Nell gave speeches. She showed charts and graphs. She pointed with her wooden pointer. More and more people gathered. More and

more money filled the jar. And then the television news crews came. And the mayor.

The mayor gave a speech in front of the cameras. Nell stood beside him. "Just this morning, our little town of Mossy Lake was unaware of the problem faced by the leopard frog. Now, thanks to Ms. Nell Foosey . . ."

Nell spoke into the microphone. "Fossey, not Foosey."

". . . we can do something about it," finished the mayor.

One of the parents stepped forward. "I'll help! I'm in the construction business. I'll donate my time for free."

"And I have a backhoe," someone else offered. "It will do the job in a jiffy."

"And I'll bring plenty of sandwiches for everyone!" Mrs. Doyle volunteered.

Nell spoke into the microphone again. "Don't forget the coffee. Decaf. Black."

The townspeople burst into cheers. The mayor shook Nell's hand. Cameras flashed. Nell was on the evening news. And on the front page of the morning paper.

Nell was a hero.

A few days later, Drake, Nell, and Dr. Livingston were back at Frog Hollow. Again Nell had her magnifying glass. "Hmm . . ." she said. A frog hopped by. "Follow that frog."

Together Drake and Nell followed the frog, with Dr. Livingston close behind. The frog hopped over a log. It hopped around a rock. It hopped through the tall grass. It hopped and hopped and hopped. And then something wonderful happened.

The frog hopped through the culvert and . . . *out the other side.*

"Oooh," whispered Drake.

"Beautiful," said Nell.

"Woof," said Dr. Livingston.

That evening, Drake wrote in his lab notebook:

*Nell* BRILLIANT.

Culvert a success.

Leopard frogs and future generations saved.

Payment zero.

PAID IN FULL.

## CHAPTER FIVE

# A DARK DAY

**I**t was a fine day for measuring tadpoles. In fact, that's exactly what Nell Fossey was doing at her desk when the phone rang. She set aside the chart she was plotting and told her tadpoles to take a break.

"Doyle and Fossey," she answered.

It was Drake. "Nell, turn your TV to Channel Five."

"Check."

She clicked on the TV. A local news reporter was talking. "We've got a situation here. A real situation. A desperate situation. As you can see behind me, a truck is wedged under the bridge. Plainly, it was just too tall. And now it's stuck. No traffic can get through, and it's miles and miles to go around. As I said, it's a desperate situation for the town of Mossy Lake."

Nell turned the TV off. "What do you suggest?"

"This is a chance for Doyle and Fossey. With our superior mental powers, we should have that truck out in a flash. Meet me at the bridge."

"Check."

*Click.*

Twenty minutes later, Nell and Drake pushed through the crowd that surrounded the truck.

"Stand back, kids," said a police officer. "Let the professionals do their jobs."

Nell handed the officer their business card. "Doyle and Fossey," she said. "At your service."

"Oh, of course, Ms. Fossey. Didn't recognize you at first. My apologies." The officer lifted the yellow tape barrier, and Nell and Drake entered the scene.

There were firefighters, engineers, and news crews. There were politicians, truck drivers, and the mayor. They stood on the bridge. They climbed on ladders. They peered under the truck with flashlights. They held meetings.

Nell set to work immediately. She observed. She measured. She calculated. She charted. She scratched her head.

Meanwhile Drake was calculating the height of the truck and scribbling in his lab notebook.

Finally, they held a small meeting of their own.

"What do you think?" Nell asked.

Drake shook his head and pushed up his glasses. "It's jammed in tight. They've already tried to drive it out, but it just wedges in further. They've tried greasing it, but no go. To be perfectly honest, I'm stumped. Simply stumped."

"Me, too."

"This is a dark day for Doyle and Fossey."

"A dark day indeed," Nell agreed.

Just then, as if being stumped weren't bad enough, they spied James Frisco. The ~~bad~~ mad scientist. Their archrival. Climbing all over the truck. Unfortunately for Doyle and Fossey, Frisco was allowed to go anywhere he liked and climb over anything he wished, because he was the police commissioner's son, mad scientist or not. Sometimes life was perfectly unfair.

Frisco peered under the hood. He checked the brakes. He squinted through the windshield. He recorded the mileage. He scribbled in his lab notebook.

And then he dashed away.

"Great Scott!" exclaimed Drake. "He's gone back

to his lab for final analysis." Drake turned to Nell. "We must solve the problem before Frisco does. Our reputation is at stake."

"Agreed."

"I have an idea that just might work," said Drake.

"Oh?"

"I'm going to raise the bridge using hot-air balloons."

Nell was quiet—real quiet. There was something not quite right here. Something she couldn't quite put her finger on. It was that sixth scientific sense that all good scientists have.

"We must return to the lab," Drake was saying, "for final analysis. And then we'll present our findings to the mayor. And we'll be home by supper."

"You go," Nell finally said. "I'm going to stay here. Just in case."

Drake thought for a moment. "Good idea. I'll watch the TV, and if anything happens I'll hurry right back."

"Check."

"Later."

## CHAPTER SIX

## SIMPLY STUMPED

**M**ossy Lake University was not too far away. In fact, it was right next door.

Nell left the scene and hurried on campus to her mother's laboratory. She often went there when she had a problem. And this was definitely a problem. Fortunately, her mother was in.

Professor Ann Fossey was sitting at her desk grading papers when Nell walked in.

"Mom?"

"Goodness gracious sakes alive, if it isn't Naturalist Nell. How are you?" And Professor Fossey hugged Nell in a most unprofessional manner. (But Nell didn't mind. Ever since her father and mother had divorced two years ago, Nell figured she needed more hugs than her normal quota. Twelve per day, to be precise.)

"What brings you here?" asked Professor Fossey.

"I have a problem. Or rather, the town has a problem."

"Really? Please explain."

And so Nell did. She explained and explained. And when she was done, she said, "So that's it. We're stumped. Simply stumped. And now Detective Doyle is going to try to raise the bridge with hot-air balloons before Frisco saves the day. I just don't know. Something's not right."

For a while neither of them spoke. Nell knew her mother was thinking hard. Her mother was always quiet when she was thinking hard. And during all this hard thinking, a clock ticked, a snake slithered, and a gerbil fell asleep.

Finally, Professor Fossey spoke. "I had a similar situation once."

"What happened?"

"I was deep in the Amazon, floating down the river. Suddenly, our canoe sprang a leak. Surrounded by crocodiles, we started sinking. It was desperate, simply desperate. It was sink or swim."

"So what did you do?" asked Nell.

"Our lead scientist suggested we quickly make friends with the monkeys. The monkeys would then swoop down from the trees and grab us just in the nick of time. But then someone else suggested that instead we hypnotize the crocodiles, using the latest techniques in animal magnetism."

"And?"

"Obviously," said Professor Fossey, "we were wasting precious time. So I simply plugged the hole with bubble gum."

"Bubble gum?" asked Nell.

"Not exactly cutting-edge science, but it worked."

"Wow," whispered Nell. But then she frowned. She didn't see the connection. "But what does this have to do with a truck stuck under a bridge?"

"Ah. Like a true scientist, you've come to the heart of the matter. You see, Nell, *sometimes the best answer is the simplest answer.* Now, I want you to return to the truck and think simple thoughts. No balloons, no grease, no peering under the hood. Here's my cell phone. If you're still stumped, give me a call here at the lab and I'll talk you through it. I know you can do it, dear." And with that, she gave Nell a quick peck on the cheek and went back to grading papers.

All the way back to the bridge, Nell puzzled over what her mother had said. *Sometimes the best answer is the simplest answer.* Crossing under the yellow tape, she surveyed the scene once again. Nothing had changed. There were still firefighters, police officers, engineers, truckers, politicians, and reporters. They still measured and jotted and held quick conferences.

Nell walked around the truck.

She scratched her head. She got real quiet. She thought real hard.

*. . . the simplest answer . . .*

And then she thought some more. It was beginning to hurt, all this thinking.

She fingered the cell phone in her jacket pocket and wondered if she should call Professor Fossey. She knew her mom would give her the answer if she asked. But no. Nell wanted to solve it herself. The answer was simple. It was right in front of her face. All she had to do was think.

And so she did. She thought simple thoughts. She thought and thought.

*. . . the simplest answer . . .*

She stared at the truck.

*. . . the truck is too tall . . .*

She stared at the tires.

And then she knew. It was simple—so simple that she was amazed no one had thought of it yet.

The answer was, of course, air pressure. The air pressure in the truck's tires supported the weight of the truck. Once that air pressure was gone, the tires would deflate, and the truck would sink.

Knowing this, Nell picked up a strong twig and calmly poked it into the valve of tire number one. (She'd seen this once on TV.)

*PSSSSSTTTTTT!!!!!*

And while no one paid her the slightest attention, she poked the twig into the valve of tire number two.

*PSSSSSTTTTTT!!!!!*

And tire number three.

*PSSSSSTTTTTT!!!!!*

By the time she had let the air out of all the tires, the entire town was watching. If they weren't there in person, they watched it on TV. Everyone gasped with amazement. It was quite impressive, really. Slowly, very slowly, the truck sank lower and lower—until, finally, it was a few inches shorter than the bridge.

"Gentleman," said Nell to the trucker, "start your engine. And next time read the height sign."

It made for a long day. All the interviews. All the handshaking with the mayor. All the explaining

about air pressure. By the time Nell returned home, her tadpoles had been waiting a very long time. They were glad to see her.

The phone rang.

"Doyle and Fossey," she said.

"Drake here. Congratulations. It was awesome. Air pressure. How did you figure it out?"

"Simple," said Nell with a satisfied sigh. "It was simple."

## CHAPTER SEVEN

# A *TEENY-TINY* CASE

**B**usiness was slow. Doyle and Fossey, Science Detectives, hadn't had a case in a week. Not even a phone call.

(The word on the streets was that Frisco was slashing his prices. No interest, no payments till next year. But that was just a rumor. If truth be known, Frisco was grounded. "No phone calls, no TV, no computer, and above all, no science for a week!" screamed his mother. "Not until you stop testing your hypotheses on your little sister!")

Rumor or no rumor, Drake didn't let slow business keep him from science. And on this particularly pleasant afternoon, he was smack-dab in the middle of a scientific breakthrough.

The phone rang.

Drake put his experiment aside. Business was business. It paid the bills. Breakthroughs would have to wait.

"Doyle and Fossey."

Nothing.

"Doyle and Fossey," Drake said again.

Finally, after what seemed ages, a tiny voice spoke. "Drake?"

"Speaking. Who is this?"

"It's Lilly. Lilly Crump." Lilly Crump was the tiniest girl in the fifth grade. Even her voice was tiny. More like a squeak.

"Oh. Hi, Lilly," said Drake as he pushed up his glasses. "Now, speak up. What seems to be the problem?"

"No problem, really. You see, I've just received an anonymous love letter. And it's my very first love letter ever. I need you to help me find out who it's from. I'm desperate."

Normally, Drake didn't take cases that involved love. After all, he couldn't measure love; he couldn't even put it in a test tube. But business was business. It paid the bills. "Check," he said. "I'll be right there."

*Click.*

Drake phoned Nell. "Meet me at Lilly's house right away, Scientist Nell. We've got a desperate case to solve and we're desperate."

"Right."

*Click.*

At Lilly's house, Drake and Nell examined the letter. They held it up to the light. They sniffed it. They peered at it through their magnifying glasses.

deer Lilly, you are prety. I lik the way you komb yer hare. you got nice frunt teath.
luv, yer sekret admiror
   P.S. its OK that yer voise skweeks

"Charming," said Nell.

"Astounding," said Drake.

"Naturally, you would want to know who sent this to you," added Nell. "Where did you find it?"

"I found it in my desk after I came in from recess today," said Lilly.

Drake pushed up his glasses. "I had a similar case once. I know just what to do. First, Nell and I will need to return to the lab. I'm afraid we'll have to take the letter."

"Evidence," said Nell.

Lilly nodded. "I understand."

"Scientist Nell and I must conduct further analysis. Expect our report within twenty-four hours," said Drake as he rushed out the door.

Back in the lab, Drake pulled a book off the shelf. He flipped through the pages until he found the right chapter: "Anonymous Letter Detection: What to do when your love life is sinking fast."

After they finished reading the chapter, Drake and Nell looked at each other.

"Looks like we'll need to go into action," said Drake.

"Check," answered Nell. "Tomorrow at school we'll gather more evidence."


The next day, Drake and Nell sat on the grass during recess. Between them lay a mound of assorted pens, each one carefully labeled.

"How did it go?" asked Nell. "Did you have any problems getting pens from everyone?"

"Only from Baloney," answered Drake. He pushed up his glasses. "When I asked to borrow his favorite pen, Baloney sat on me and threatened to squeeze my eyes out. Fortunately, when he left, his pen was lying on the floor beside me."

"Wow," whispered Nell. "The dangers of science."

Baloney was the biggest kid in the fifth grade. Even his elbows were big. (His real name was Bubba

Mahoney, but everyone called him Baloney.) Usually Drake used his good scientific sense and stayed away from Baloney, but business was business. Drake knew that a good scientist must put aside his emotions and stick to his goal. Even if it means being sat on.

"Now," said Drake, "it is obvious to me that since the letter was written in black ballpoint ink, we can immediately remove all the pens that aren't black. How many does that leave us?"

"Hmm . . . a moment, please." Nell tested the pens on a piece of scrap paper. "Out of the original twenty-eight pens, we are left with nineteen."

"Hmm . . . nine down, nineteen to go."

"Affirmative."

Once school was out, Drake and Nell rushed to the laboratory. All afternoon they worked. They cut long strips of paper. They labeled each strip.

*Elliot Zelder,* Nell wrote across the top of one strip, using the pen labeled ELLIOT ZELDER. On the bottom of the same strip, she drew a heavy dot.

*Baloney,* wrote Drake on another strip with Bubba Mahoney's pen.

*James Frisco,* Nell wrote with Frisco's pen.

And so on . . .

When all the strips were labeled, they hung the bottom of each strip in separate beakers of alcohol.

Finally, they cut a strip from the love letter. At the bottom of the love-letter strip was the heart, drawn in black ink. They suspended the end in another beaker of alcohol.

And then they waited. And waited. And waited.

"Hot chocolate?" asked Mrs. Doyle as she peeked into the lab.

"No thanks," said Drake. "Just muffins."

"Coffee. Decaf. Black," said Nell.

"Affirmative," replied Mrs. Doyle. And soon she returned with muffins and a steaming cup of coffee.

Then, as Drake and Nell watched, rainbows of colors slowly crept up the strips of paper. Purples, reds, golds, pinks, and blues. It was really quite pretty.

Finally, Drake and Nell compared the different strips to the strip cut from Lilly's love letter. "Analysis complete," said Drake. "Out of the nineteen strips we tested, only two match the ink in the love letter."

Nell scratched her head, obviously thinking hard. "One of the matching strips belongs to the spelling bee champion. And the love letter was filled with spelling errors, so it couldn't possibly be him. Which means that . . ."

Drake and Nell gasped with surprise as they read the name on the last matching strip. ". . . we've found our man," they said together.

## CHAPTER EIGHT

## DESPERATE MEASURES

**M**eanwhile, Lilly Crump waited at her house. And waited. And waited.

Why don't they call? she thought. She wrung her hands. She paced the floor. She stared out the window. You see, Lilly Crump was lonely. She had no brothers or sisters. She didn't even have a dog or cat. All she had was an itty-bitty fish with buggy eyes. So when the phone finally rang, Lilly leaped to answer. "Hello?" Her heart was pounding.

"Lilly?"

Lilly recognized Drake's voice. "Yes?"

"We've got your answer, Ms. Crump. Come to the lab immediately."

"I'll be right there," squeaked Lilly.

Lilly was true to her word. Within five minutes she arrived. "I ran the whole way," she gasped. "Now tell me before I die. Who is it? Who's in love with me?"

Drake pushed up his glasses. "Observe," he said, pointing to the strips of paper. "Inks are not all the same."

"Certainly not," agreed Nell.

"An ink may look black—" said Drake.

"—or blue," added Nell.

"But they are in fact made of many different colors. Nell and I separated the colors in a process called chromatography. It's quite simple, really. As alcohol moves through the ink, the different colors separate."

"That's because," Nell explained, "the different colors do not have the same weight. They move faster or slower depending upon how heavy they are." She pointed at the strips of paper with her long wooden pointer. "As you can see, each ink is like a fingerprint. All we had to do was match the ink in the letter—"

"—with the ink in the paper strips," finished Drake proudly. "And each strip is carefully labeled, so we know whose pen it was."

"And?" asked Lilly, her eyes wide. "Whose was it? Who wrote me the letter?"

Drake and Nell glanced at each other.

Drake swallowed hard. "You tell her," he said.

Nell took a deep breath. "I think you'd better sit down."

Lilly sat. She could hardly wait.

"It was Baloney," Nell finally blurted. "Bubba Baloney Mahoney."

Suddenly there was a silence. A deep silence. A deep, dark silence. A deep, dark, dreadful silence.

Drake couldn't stand it any longer. He shook Lilly's shoulders. "Snap out of it!" he ordered.

Lilly didn't respond. Instead, she slid off the stool like a wet noodle and fell to the floor.

Drake was desperate. He knew that if he didn't do something soon, Lilly might go into shock. After that, a coma. After that . . . well, he knew that whatever it was, it would be quite awful. "Quick, Scientist Nell!" hollered Drake. "Pour a beaker of water over Ms. Crump's head! There's not a second to lose!"

"Check!"

*Sploosh!*

"*Splutter!*"

Dazed and drowned, Lilly stared at them.

"Speak!" ordered Drake.

"Oh, Baloney!" Lilly said. She clasped her hands together.

"Huh?" Drake and Nell looked at her in astonishment.

"Thank you, Detective Doyle and Scientist Nell. Thank you! This is the happiest day of my life!" Lilly gave each of them a teeny-tiny hug.

Drake returned the love letter, along with a business card. "Call us. Anytime."

"Oh, I will! I will!" Then Lilly flew out of the room as fast as her little legs could carry her.

After she was gone, Nell shook her head. "There are some things science can't explain."

"Indeed, Scientist Nell," Drake said. "Indeed."

That evening, Drake wrote in his lab notebook:

Love letter mystery solved.
Baloney the culprit.
Don't understand this thing
called **LOVE**.
(A MYSTERY.)
Received one fish with Buggy eyes
as payment—MUST RETURN in
one week.
PAID IN FULL.

# Activities and Experiments for Super-Scientists

## Contents

# Your Own Lab

**D**o you want to perform experiments just like Drake Doyle and Nell Fossey? Create your own laboratory—it's easy!

**❶** Start by collecting beakers and flasks. Clear glass bottles and jars work great. Wash thoroughly, and remove old labels by soaking them in warm, soapy water. Any time an experiment calls for a beaker, use a jar. For flasks, use bottles.

**❷** Keep a lab notebook. Any notebook will do. Lab notebooks are important because they tell you what you've done. (Imagine a scientist who wonders how he did whatchamacallit experiment last year. Instead of guessing, he looks it up in his lab notebook! Ta-da! Complete with coffee stains!)

### A good lab notebook contains

1) experiment title
2) method
   (what you plan to do)
3) hypothesis
   (what you think
   will happen)

4) procedure
   (what you did)
5) observations
   (what you saw)
6) results
   (what actually happened)

**❸** Find a lab coat. Lab coats protect your clothes and skin from chemicals. (Plus, they're spiffy.) Large white button-down shirts with the sleeves rolled up work well. If you can't find one around your house (ask first!), they're available at secondhand clothing stores. Using a permanent marker, write your name on it.

# Method to the Madness

**I**n the story "Monster Mission," Drake and Nell used the **scientific method.** Based on their observations of the garbage can, they developed a **hypothesis.** A hypothesis is a statement that explains what you think is really happening. In other words, a hypothesis is an educated guess. Drake's hypothesis might have sounded something like this:

> ### Based on my observations, I believe yeast is growing in the garbage can.

But a scientist doesn't stop with a hypothesis. A hypothesis may or may not be correct. The only way for a scientist to find out is to perform experiments to test the hypothesis, just as Drake and Nell did. The steps taken to test a hypothesis are known as a **procedure.** These are the instructions you'll follow as you perform experiments and activities similar to Drake and Nell's. Put on your lab coat, wash your hands, and stick a pencil behind your ear, because here we go!

### Good Science Tip

Read through the instructions and set out all needed materials before beginning the experiment. Use only clean equipment. Record each step of the experiment's procedure in your lab notebook.

# Mr. Talberg's Famous Bread Recipe

### (And one not-so-famous bread recipe)

**T**hat's right! Here's Mr. Talberg's recipe, famous all over Mossy Lake; soon to be famous in your town, too. (CAUTION: This is a highly delicious activity, and it takes about two hours.)

(TOP-SECRET: This is also a top-secret operation, but it's so cleverly disguised that your poor, unsuspecting family *won't even know it.*)

## Materials

- two medium-size bowls
- measuring spoons and cups
- flour
- sugar
- salt
- butter or margarine
- warm water: 105°–120°F (about as hot as bathwater)
- two miniature bread pans
- cooking oil spray
- masking tape and marker
- dish towel
- 1 ¼-oz. package quick-rising yeast

**Note:** Check the expiration date on the yeast. It is a living (yikes! it's *alive!*) plant and is able to survive for one year in a dried (dehydrated) state. Yeast is found in nature, even in the air we breathe! Yeast is activated by warmth and moisture, much as seeds are activated when planted and watered. If it's past the expiration date, the yeast will not activate. Also, make certain it's *quick-rising* yeast. It should say so on the label.

## Procedure

**❶** Turn on your oven light and close the oven door. This will create a warm environment for the yeast to grow. (Oven should be OFF. Light should be ON.)

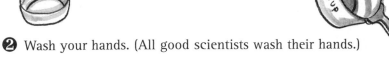

**②** Wash your hands. (All good scientists wash their hands.)

**③** Into *each* bowl, measure 1½ cups flour, 1 tablespoon sugar, ½ teaspoon salt, and 1 teaspoon butter or margarine.

**④** Add ½ teaspoon yeast to *one* of the bowls containing the flour mixture. Label the bowl YEAST. Mix well.

**⑤** Add ½ cup warm water into *each* bowl. Stir until a good dough forms. Pick up each dough ball with your hands (one at a time) and squeeze it for several minutes, working it back and forth. (Squoosh, moosh, squeeze, and tease.) If it's too gooey, add a little more flour. Let each dough ball sit for 10 minutes.

**⑥** After 10 minutes, form each dough ball into a loaf shape and put into a greased miniature bread pan. Label the bread pan containing the yeast, YEAST. (Like, duh.)

**⑦** Set both loaves in your oven and cover them with a dish towel. Close the door. (Your oven should be OFF, but the oven light should be ON.) Set the timer for one hour.

**❽** Relax. (SOME IDEAS FOR RELAXING: Lie in a hammock, pester your mother, call your best friend, play solitaire, jog in place, study Einstein's theory of relativity.)

**❾** Once the timer goes off, remove dish towel from the loaves. Now turn on oven and bake loaves at 350°F for 40–45 minutes, or until golden brown. (The one without the yeast may be pale, hard, and ugly, but that's the way it goes.)

**❿** Serve your unsuspecting family *both* loaves of bread. Pretend you don't notice the difference. Later, write down their reactions in your lab notebook and draw your conclusions regarding yeast. (EXAMPLES OF REACTIONS: Amazing! Delicious! Mouthwatering! Three cheers for the cook! OR: Disgusting! Ow, I broke my tooth! Who made this stuff anyway?)

**Disclaimer**

Not responsible for broken teeth or hard, lumpy cases of indigestion. You didn't hear it from us.

# Send a Secret Message

**H**ow did Nell write Drake a secret message in Chapter Three? Find out by writing a secret message of your own.

## Materials

- lemon juice
- cotton swab

- blank piece of notebook paper
- lamp with 100-watt bulb

## Procedure

**❶** Pour a little lemon juice into a small bowl.

**❷** Dip the cotton swab into the lemon juice.

**❸** Using the swab like a pen, write a message on the paper. Make sure you use plenty of lemon juice. Dip as often as needed.

**❹** Allow the paper to dry completely.

**❺** To read the message, switch on a lamp and wait until the light-bulb is very warm. Hold the paper close to it until the letters appear. It will take a minute or so. (Be careful, as the paper could catch on fire if it gets too hot! Have an adult help if you are unsure.)

### How does this work?

Paper soaked in lemon juice burns at a lower temperature than regular paper. The lemon-juice letters scorch, turning brown, while the rest of the paper stays mostly white.

# Emergency! Naturalists Needed! Help Save the Frogs!

**A**ll young naturalists around the globe, listen up! Nell Fossey here. We've got a major situation, and time is running out.

Here's the scoop. The world population of frogs is decreasing. That's right, the poor little frogs of the world are disappearing fast, and it's up to us to save them. (After all, if we don't save them, who will?)

Why are they disappearing? you ask. Good question. Let me think...how about ozone depletion, global warming, pollution, pesticides, habitat destruction, and acid rain for starters? Need I go on? I didn't think so.

I've made a list of what you can do to help. Even if you don't live in a froggy area, there's plenty on the list for you to do. It's a desperate situation. Calling all naturalists to the rescue!

**Nell's tips on what YOU can do to SAVE THE FROGS:**

1. Build a frog pond.

> FIND OUT HOW TO BUILD A FROG POND:
>
> http://www.nwf.org/habitats/index.html
>
> http://www.acfonline.org.au/earthkids/frogdrm.htm
>
> http://host4u.upws.net/frogweb/ponds.html

2. Plant a tree.

I need moisture and shade to survive.

My froggy skin absorbs chemicals. Yuck!

3. Become frog-smart regarding chemicals:
   - Encourage your family to use organic (natural) lawn and garden products.
   - Use cleaning products labeled "biodegradable," which means they break down naturally.
   - Dispose of hazardous wastes, such as paints, solvents, motor oil, etc., through your local waste-management center. DO NOT pour them down the drain or dump them in your backyard, because they will end up in your local lakes, rivers, and streams.

Compost is frog friendly.

4. Start a compost pile. Compost is a biodegradable, natural fertilizer that plants (and frogs!) love.

---

FIND OUT HOW TO START A COMPOST PILE:

http://aggie-horticulture.tamu.edu/sustainable/
slidesets/kidscompost/cover.html

http://www.dnr.state.wi.us/org/caer/ce/eek/
earth/compost.htm

---

5. Make sure your air conditioner doesn't leak Freon. Freon depletes (eats away) the ozone layer, letting too much UV radiation through.

Radiation can hurt our eggs.

Uh-oh. I'm feeling SICK.

6. If you want to raise a tadpole, collect only a few frog eggs and take good care of them. If you release them, do that ONLY where you found them. NEVER release your frogs or tadpoles anyplace else; otherwise they may introduce new parasites (nasty germs and creepy-crawlies) into the frogs that already live there.

7. Write your government representatives and ask them to preserve wetlands and to support the Endangered Species Act.

8. Encourage your classroom to adopt a local stream or pond. Make a commitment to keep that stream or pond clean.

9. Volunteer to help the government monitor the frog population.

CONTACT:

http://www.mp2-pwrc.usgs.gov/frogwatch

OR WRITE:

Frogwatch USA Coordinator, Patuxent Wildlife Research Center, 12100 Beech Forest Road, Room 242 Gabrielson Lab, Laurel, MD 20708-4038

(301) 497-5819

Frog Friends of the world, unite!

10. Join an organization to help care for animals and the environment.

SOME ORGANIZATIONS TO CONTACT:

Rainforest Action Network, http://www.ran.org

221 Pine St., Ste. 500, San Francisco, CA 94104

(415) 398-4404

World Wildlife Fund

http://www.worldwildlife.org

1250 24th St., NW, P.O. Box 97180,

Washington, D.C. 20037  1-800-CALL-WWF

National Wildlife Federation

http://www.nwf.org

8925 Leesburg Pike, Vienna, VA 22184. (703) 790-4000

Has the Web site moved? Search for similar Web sites by using a search engine on the World Wide Web and typing combinations of words, such as FROGS KIDS or FROGS KIDS ENVIRONMENT or SAVE FROGS KIDS. You'll find all kinds of froggy information!

## Did you know?

Every year in Britain, about 300,000 toads get squashed while trying to cross the road to reach their breeding grounds. To help the situation, volunteers spend their evenings loading the toads into buckets and carrying them across the roads.

Toadally amazing!! You're my heroes!!

# Hang on to Your Hats!

**I**t's hard to believe that air can be so powerful. Tornadoes whirl trucks, houses, and people right off the ground! (Chickens, too!) Hurricanes knock over trees as if they were twigs.

But those are forces of nature, and everybody knows that tornadoes and hurricanes are powerful. How about something as little as your breath? Maybe your breath can blow out a few birthday candles, but could it hold up a truck?

Believe it or not, if you had *enough* of your breath, you *could* hold up a truck. When enough air is squished (compressed) into a limited space, such as a tire, it becomes very strong and can hold up a car or a tractor or a semitrailer.

Want to amaze your friends with your newfound knowledge? Practice the following activity first, and then ask your friends if they can lift a stack of books using just their breath. After they stop laughing, show them how it's done!

## Materials

- books
- big balloon

## Procedure

Set the stack of books on a table and hide the balloon under the books. Make sure the neck of the balloon is sticking out. Without removing the balloon, blow it up. Voilà!

68

# A Most Mysterious Case

**Y**ou have been assigned a most mysterious case. The case of the...(gasp)...*Mysterious Black Dot!*

The Scene: You have assembled five black ballpoint pens. Although the pens are different brands, their inks look identical. While your back is turned, your friend draws a heavy dot (•) on a piece of white paper with one of the pens. (Why, you ask? Why would your friend do such a mysterious thing? Because you asked him to, that's why.)

The Problem: You do not know which pen he used.

The Mission: Using chromatography, find out which pen your friend used.

## Materials

- 5 black ballpoint pens (different brands)
- masking tape
- scissors
- plain white paper

- 6 beakers
- measuring spoon
- rubbing alcohol
- clear tape

## Procedure

❶ Label the pens 1 through 5, using masking tape.

❷ Cut 5 strips of paper the same height as the beakers and ½ inch wide. Label the strips 1 through 5 across the top.

❸ Pour 1 tablespoon of alcohol into each beaker. (CAUTION: Alcohol is flammable, which means it can catch on fire easily. Keep it away from flame.)

For **each** pen, do steps 4 and 5, starting with pen #1 and strip #1:

**❹** With pen #1, draw a heavy dot (•) one inch from the bottom of strip #1. The darker the dot, the better.

**❺** Tape the top of strip #1 to pen #1, using clear tape. Hang the strip in the beaker by resting the pen across the mouth of the beaker. The bottom of the strip should dip in the alcohol, but the dot of ink should be *above* the alcohol.

**❻** Cut out a strip of paper containing the mysterious black dot. Like the other strips, the black dot should measure one inch from the bottom of the strip. Label the top of the strip "M," for "mysterious." Tape the strip to a spare pencil and hang in the sixth beaker of alcohol.

**❼** Take a major break. (MAJOR BREAK IDEAS: Dust for fingerprints, clean your spy glasses, snoop around corners.)

❽ After 4 hours, remove the strips. Which ink matches the "mysterious" ink? Show your friend the evidence. Were you right? (When his mouth flaps open in surprise, say: "Aha! I knew it all along! You can't fool me! Easy-schmeasy!")

❾ Tape the dried strips into your lab notebook. This is your hard evidence.

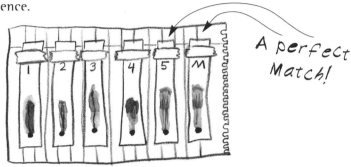

A perfect Match!

❿ IMPORTANT: DO NOT pour the leftover alcohol down the drain. Instead, use a funnel to pour the alcohol into a clean, dry bottle. Label the bottle RUBBING ALCOHOL and ask an adult to safely store it for a future experiment.

## Did You Know?

Did you know that the FBI uses chromatography to catch forgers? (A forger is someone who writes a fake document.) By testing the ink on a document, detectives can determine the type, the age, and even the manufacturer of the ink. (It is impossible for a document to be, say, fifty years old if the ink in the document was made just last year!)